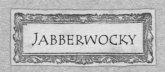

JABBERWOCKY

FOR
PETE AND LEO

J. S.

Lewis Carroll

Jabber

First published 2003 by Walker Books Ltd
87 Vauxhall Walk, London SE11 5HJ

2 4 6 8 10 9 7 5 3 1

Illustrations © 2003 Joel Stewart

This book has been typeset in Veljovic and Tempus.

Printed in Italy

British Library Cataloguing in Publication Data:
a catalogue record for this book is available
from the British Library

ISBN 0-7445-9293-3

WOCKY

ILLUSTRATED BY

JOEL STEWART

WALKER BOOKS
AND SUBSIDIARIES
LONDON • BOSTON • SYDNEY

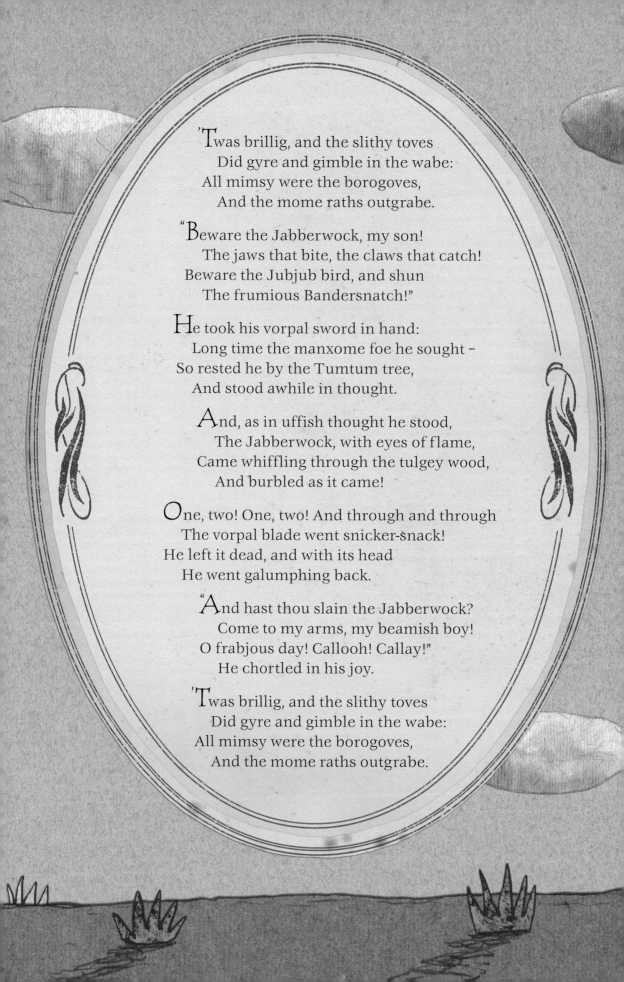

'Twas brillig, and the slithy toves
    Did gyre and gimble in the wabe:
All mimsy were the borogoves,
    And the mome raths outgrabe.

"Beware the Jabberwock, my son!
    The jaws that bite, the claws that catch!
Beware the Jubjub bird, and shun
    The frumious Bandersnatch!"

He took his vorpal sword in hand:
    Long time the manxome foe he sought –
So rested he by the Tumtum tree,
    And stood awhile in thought.

And, as in uffish thought he stood,
    The Jabberwock, with eyes of flame,
Came whiffling through the tulgey wood,
    And burbled as it came!

One, two! One, two! And through and through
    The vorpal blade went snicker-snack!
He left it dead, and with its head
    He went galumphing back.

"And hast thou slain the Jabberwock?
    Come to my arms, my beamish boy!
O frabjous day! Callooh! Callay!"
    He chortled in his joy.

'Twas brillig, and the slithy toves
    Did gyre and gimble in the wabe:
All mimsy were the borogoves,
    And the mome raths outgrabe.

'TWAS BRILLIG,

AND THE

SLITHY TOVES

DID
GYRE
AND
GIMBLE
IN THE
WABE:

ALL MIMSY

WERE THE

BOROGOVES,

AND THE
MOME RATHS
OUTGRABE.

HE TOOK

HIS VORPAL SWORD

IN HAND:

LONG TIME

THE MANXOME

FOE HE SOUGHT –

So rested

he by the

Tumtum tree,

AND STOOD AWHILE IN THOUGHT.

AND, AS IN

UFFISH THOUGHT

HE STOOD,

THE JABBERWOCK,

WITH EYES

OF FLAME,

CAME
WHIFFLING
THROUGH THE
TULGEY WOOD,
AND BURBLED
AS IT CAME!

ONE, TWO!

ONE, TWO!

AND THROUGH

AND THROUGH

THE VORPAL

BLADE WENT

SNICKER–SNACK!

HE LEFT IT DEAD,

AND WITH ITS HEAD

HE WENT

GALUMPHING BACK.

"AND HAST THOU SLAIN

THE JABBERWOCK?

COME TO MY ARMS,

MY BEAMISH BOY!

O FRABJOUS DAY!

CALLOOH! CALLAY!"

HE CHORTLED

IN HIS JOY.

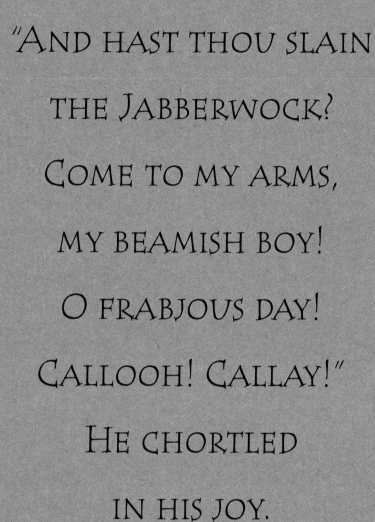

'TWAS BRILLIG, AND
THE SLITHY TOVES
DID GYRE AND GIMBLE
IN THE WABE:

All mimsy were

the borogoves,

And the mome raths

outgrabe.